This Walker book belongs to:

_____

_____

To my Popie, for teaching me how to draw a star all those years ago.

And to my boys, Ben and Jack, for inspiring the song that became the story.

Have another milkshake for the road…

K. N.

To my granddaughter, Nana, who always cheers me up with

her adorable smile, and to my husband, Ko, for all his support.

This book is for them with deepest gratitude.

C. O.

WALKER BOOKS
AND SUBSIDIARIES
LONDON · BOSTON · SYDNEY · AUCKLAND

First published in Great Britain 2019 by Walker Books Ltd • 87 Vauxhall Walk, London SE11 5HJ • This edition published 2020 • Text © 2018 Karl Newson Illustrations © 2018 Chiaki Okada • The right of Karl Newson and Chiaki Okada to be identified as the author and illustrator of this work respectively has been asserted by them in accordance with the Copyright, Designs and Patents Act 1988 • Published by arrangement with Paper Crane Agency • This book has been typeset in Alice • Printed in China • All rights reserved. No part of this book may be reproduced, transmitted or stored in an information retrieval system in any form or by any means, graphic, electronic or mechanical, including photocopying, taping and recording, without prior written permission from the publisher. • British Library Cataloguing in Publication Data: a catalogue record for this book is available from the British Library • ISBN 978-1-4063-8306-5 • www.walker.co.uk • 10 9 8 7 6 5 4 3 2 1

For All the Stars Across the Sky

Karl Newson   illustrated by Chiaki Okada

At the end of the day,
when the sun is fading
and Luna is yawning . . .

it's time for pyjamas,
teeth brushing
and climbing into bed.

"Now close your eyes," says Mum,
"and we'll make a wish . . .

For all the stars across the sky,
Big and little and bright,
Here's a wish from me to you,
Before we say goodnight."

"I wish," says Luna,
"that we could fly like birds!"

"So let's be birds!" says Mum.
"Let's fly by mountaintops
and patchwork fields,
just you, the clouds and me."

"All the way around the world," says Luna,
"and over the deep blue sea…"

"Now I wish we could swim like fish!"

"Let's dip and dive," says Mum,
"in corals made of every colour,
just you, the whale song and me."

"Oh, wow!" says Luna. "I feel so small..."

"Now I wish we were even smaller –
like ladybirds!"

"Let's catch a ride," says Mum,
"exploring the vines
and the twigs in the mud,
just you, the crickets and me."

"Let's creep and climb!" says Luna.
"To the top of a dandelion that's as high
as the sky . . . oh, I know!
Shall we be big again?"

"I wish we were big, really big –
like giants!"

"Let's gaze over treetops," says Mum,
"and stomp loudly down the lane,
just you, the birds and me…"

"Let's *stomp, stomp, stomp* all the way
home to our giant's house,
because even giants sleep sometimes."

"And our giant's bed is just the right size,"
says Luna. "Just the right size
for you and me."

At the end of the day,
when the sun is fading
and Luna's eyes are closing,
it's time for turning out the lights,
snuggling into bed
and dreaming sweet dreams…

"For all the stars across the sky,

Big and little and bright,

Here's a kiss from me to you,

As we say goodnight."

Karl Newson is a children's author whose picture books include *A Bear is a Bear*, illustrated by Anuska Allepuz, *The Same But Different Too*, illustrated by Kate Hindley and *I Am A Tiger*, illustrated by Ross Collins. Karl lives in London, and you can find him online at karlnewson.com, on Twitter as @Karlwheel and on Instagram as @karl_newson.

Chiaki Okada is a Japanese artist and illustrator who has worked with authors from across the world, including her husband, author Ko Okada, with whom she created *Is That You, Spring?* and *My First Night Away*. *For All the Stars Across the Sky* is her first picture book published in English.
You can find Chiaki online at okada-chiaki.com.